Clottus and the
Ghostly Gladiator

ROMANS by Ann Jungman & Mike Phillips

Bacillus and the Beastly Bath
Clottus and the Ghostly Gladiator
Tertius and the Horrible Hunt
Twitta and the Ferocious Fever

First paperback edition 2002
First published 2002 in hardback by
A & C Black (Publishers) Ltd
37 Soho Square, London W1D 3QZ

ISBN 0-7136-5958-0

A CIP catalogue record for this book is available
from the British Library.

Printed and bound by G. Z. Printek, Bilbao, Spain.

ROMANS

Clottus
and the
Ghostly Gladiator

ANN JUNGMAN

ILLUSTRATED BY
MIKE PHILLIPS

A & C BLACK • LONDON

CHAPTER 1
Flying

'Oh, Clottus, not again! You Romans! I don't know, when it comes to horse-riding you're useless.'

'I do try to stay on, Gorjus, really I do, but it's very hard,' said Clottus, rubbing the bump on his head.

'Well, your father says I've got to teach you to ride a horse properly, so up you get and climb back on that horse now!'

'Don't want to,' grumbled Clottus, 'and I don't see why I should have to do what you say. After all, you're only a slave, Gorjus.'

Gorjus picked Clottus up and put him back on his horse. 'It's not what I say, Master Clottus, it's what your father says. Now, off you go. And do try not to fall on your head again or you'll be even dafter than you are already.'

'I don't know what you mean, Gorjus.'

'Never mind,' sighed Gorjus. 'Come to think of it, there's no way you could be any dafter than you are, so fall off any way you like, head, feet, bottom — take your choice. Go on, away with you!' Gorjus gave the horse a slap and it galloped off.

'Help!' yelled Clottus, as the horse disappeared over a hedge with its young Roman master clinging on for dear life.

Twitta, Clottus's sister, found Gorjus bent double with laughter. 'What's so funny, Gorjus?' said Twitta.

'Oh, hello there, Mistress Twitta,' smiled the slave. 'It's your twin brother, mistress. That boy just can't manage to stay on his horse.'

Twitta knew how hopeless Clottus was on a horse, and giggled too. 'Do you know where he is, Gorjus? Father wants him.'

'Clottus went off in that direction, Mistress Twitta. Over that hedge there. Let's go and look for him. He'll be lying head down in a cowpat somewhere is my guess.'

Gorjus and Twitta climbed through the hedge. There was the horse happily eating grass. And he didn't have a rider.

'He's not here,' cried Twitta. 'Father will be so cross. Oh Clottus, where are you?'

'Here!' came a voice. 'Up here in the tree. I'm stuck. Help! Get me out of here! Quickly!'

Twitta and Gorjus looked up. There, high up in an oak tree, hung Clottus, waving his legs and arms madly.

'Master Clottus,' laughed Gorjus, 'you are supposed to be learning to ride, not to fly.' He shinned up the tree to release Clottus, and dropped him gently onto the ground.

'What happened?' asked Twitta.

'That's one very mean horse and he's got it in for me,' said Clottus. 'He waited till we were under the oak tree and then he just threw me,' he complained. 'I shall never ride that horse again — never, never, ever! Gorjus, you will have to tell my father that the horse is a freak.'

'We'll see about that, Master Clottus. Now, I'm going to fetch the horse and the three of us can ride him back to the house.'

'Never,' said Clottus stubbornly, sitting on the grass and folding his arms. 'Never, ever will I get on that horse again.'

'You'll be quite safe, this horse won't dare play me up. Off we go. Wave to your dad, Master Clottus, that's right... now smile. Make it look as though you've had the best day of your life, or we're both in trouble.'

CHAPTER 2

Ruined

'So, Clottus, how did the riding lesson go?'
asked Marcellus, his father.

'Fine,' said Clottus.
'Terrific, Father,' agreed Twitta.

'I see. So why are you covered in cuts and bruises and mud, Clottus, and — if my nose is right — something even worse?'

'The horse went mad, Father. It wasn't my fault, anyone would have fallen off.'

'Oh dear,' sighed Marcellus. 'Is my son ever going to learn to ride, Gorjus?'

'Oh yes, master. I'll see that he has a good seat on a horse, if it's the last thing I do.'

'Good. He'll never ride like you, though, Gorjus. You Dacians seem to be born in the saddle.'

'True, master. I learned to ride before I could walk. If you grow up on the wide plains you have to.'

'Where is Dacia, Gorjus?' asked Twitta.

A far-away look came into Gorjus's eyes. 'Right at the other end of the Roman Empire, Mistress Twitta — almost as far as you can go to the east,' he said.

'I'll show you on a map, Twitta,' said her father. 'Clottus, go and wash and then join us in my study.'

Marcellus turned to his slave. 'There is some trouble with the cattle, Gorjus. Go and help the other slaves, please. You're so good with the animals.'

'Nothing serious, I hope, master?'

'Let's hope not.'

Gorjus looked alarmed. 'But master, on this estate we're so dependent on selling the cows' milk, if it's the cattle sickness people are talking about, then that's really bad.'

'Yes, and I'd be in deep trouble, deep, deep trouble. So pray to your gods, Gorjus, whoever they are, that it's nothing to worry about.'

'I will, master, I will,' agreed Gorjus and he walked away to the cattle shed with a worried look on his face.

'Are you going to show me where Gorjus comes from on the map, or not?' asked Twitta, tugging at her father's hand.

'Of course, come on.'

'Dacia is here, Twitta.'

'I see, and where are we?'

'We are in Verulamium in Britain, and Rome is where your mother and I come from.'

'And all this shaded land belongs to Rome?'

'That's right.'

'So we Romans are in charge?'

'We certainly are.'

At that moment Gorjus ran in. 'Yes, what is it?' asked Marcellus. 'I just want a bit of time on my own with my daughter without being so rudely interrupted. It had better be important, Gorjus, or I'll have you whipped.'

'It is important, master. Bad news! The cows have the cattle pest. They will all have to be killed.'

Marcellus turned white. 'Oh no!' he cried, struggling to his feet. 'I'm ruined, Gorjus! What can I do now?'

'Take Twitta to her mother, Gorjus, while I gather my wits.'

Twitta followed Gorjus out of her father's study.

'Gorjus,' she asked him, 'why did you leave your home in Dacia to come so far away and live with us?'

'It wasn't my choice, Mistress Twitta. I was captured by the Romans in battle and forced to be a slave. Your father bought me and brought me here.'

'Do you miss your home?'

'Of course I do, every day. I miss being free to ride like the wind across the wide open plains.'

'Poor Gorjus,' said Twitta, squeezing his hand. 'But we're glad you're here.'

CHAPTER 3

For Sale

'Gorjus,' said Clottus a few days later, 'Twitta says you were captured by us Romans and sold as a slave.'

'What of it?' asked Gorjus. 'Why did you let yourself get captured? Why didn't you just jump on your horse and ride off to safety?'

'I got an arrow in my leg. Look, here's the scar. I rode and rode but eventually I bled so much that I fell off and got captured.'

'That's a very big scar, Gorjus,' said Clottus sympathetically. 'I bet it hurt.'

'Terribly,' admitted Gorjus. 'And I still get a twinge when it rains, which, as you know, it does rather often.'

'Poor Gorjus,' said Clottus. 'But Twitta and I, we're really, really glad you're here. You won't ever leave us will you, Gorjus?'

'No, young master, not unless your father decides to sell me.'

'He wouldn't do that,' Clottus told the slave. 'What a daft idea.'

'It's not impossible, you know. He may have to, with all the cattle dying. A young, healthy slave is worth a lot of money.'

'Don't worry, Gorjus, Twitta and I won't let him.'

Clottus and Gorjus were beginning
the walk to school, when
Marcellus called out,
'Clottus, Gorjus!
Come here a minute.'

'Master Clottus will be
late for school, master.'

'I know, but this is important,' Marcellus
told them. 'I hate to tell you this, but I am
going to have to sell some of the slaves.
Gorjus, I'm sorry but you will be one of them.
Now the cattle are all destroyed, I can't afford
to keep you. On Saturday, I will take you to
the slave market and I promise I'll only sell you
to a kind master.'

'But Father, you can't!' implored Clottus, horrified. 'Gorjus is like family. You can't sell him, you don't have the right.'

'Oh, but I do,' replied Marcellus sharply. 'And Clottus, if you go on, I'll put you up for sale too.'

'You can't, you're not allowed to. I'm your son,' muttered Clottus.

'And I am your father, the head of this household, and I can do what I like. I can sell you, or kill you, or lock you up — don't you forget it. Now off you go to school, I've got a lot on my mind.'

Seeing his son's miserable expression Marcellus relented slightly. 'And Clottus, it breaks my heart to do this, but it's necessary, and I don't want to hear any more about it.'

Clottus and Gorjus walked on to school in silence.

At the school Gorjus gave Clottus a big hug. 'Goodbye, Master Clottus. Take care and learn to ride a horse for me.'

'Gorjus, I'll be home later. I'll see you before they take you away. Oh, Gorjus, I'll miss you so much. You're my favourite person in the whole wide world.'

CHAPTER 4

Disappeared

That day Clottus walked home from school
alone. 'Gorjus didn't come and meet me,' he
complained to his mother, Deleria.

'He's upset about being sold,' Deleria told
Clottus. 'But don't worry, I've talked your
father out of it. I've got some money to tide us
over. Your father panicked unnecessarily.'

'Oh Mother, that's the best news.'

His mother smiled at him. 'Well, don't waste time! Go and find Gorjus and tell him the good news yourself.'

Clottus found Twitta and together they looked for Gorjus. But though they searched all the rest of the day, there was no sign of him.

'Don't you worry,' said Perpendicula, the cook, when they asked in the kitchen. 'He likes his food, does Gorjus. He'll be back here for his dinner.'

But night fell, and still there was no Gorjus.

'Looks like he's run away rather than be sold,' said Marcellus to Deleria.

'Well I don't blame him,' replied his wife. 'And look at the children, they're so miserable they're not eating a thing.'

'All right, you two,' groaned Marcellus. 'I'm sorry. Tomorrow we'll go and look for Gorjus — he can't have gone far. Cheer up. We'll soon find him, that's for sure. And I've got the papers ready to make him a freeman.'

But the next day they searched all the local farms and villages and even went right to Verulamium, but there was no sign of Gorjus.

'I'll ride on down the Watling Way to
Londinium and see if he's gone that way,'
cried Marcellus, but although he searched
and searched there was still no sign of Gorjus.

'I'm sorry, children,' Marcellus told them both later that night, 'but poor old Gorjus must have gone off into the forest and been eaten by a bear or a wolf. I wish I hadn't been so hasty. Please forgive me.'

But the children moped around and stopped eating.

'I can't stand this,' said Marcellus after a few days. 'I'm going to talk to your mother.'

But Deleria just lay on her couch and wept.

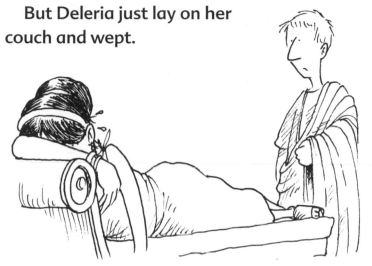

'I'll go and make sure the slaves are getting on with things,' thought Marcellus, but the slaves were all in mourning as well.

'I'm going to take a ride on my horse,' grumbled Marcellus to the world in general, but even the horse was miserable. So Marcellus sat in the garden and threw a ball for the dogs, but the dogs just lay there with their heads on their paws, and whimpered.

That night Marcellus had to eat alone. 'Just me and the statues,' he thought.

'At least they won't cry on me.' Just then he looked up and saw a tear run down the face of a statue.

'This has got to stop!' yelled Marcellus. The noise brought the cook running. 'All because of some wretched slave. I can't stand this. Go and fetch my wife and children, Perpendicula, I've got something to say to them.'

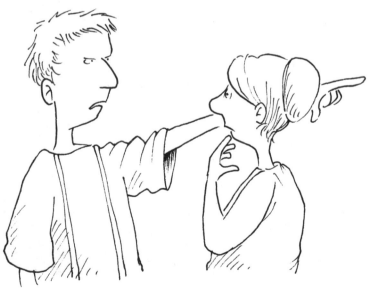

Deleria, Clottus and Twitta appeared at the door.

'Wife, children,' said Marcellus, 'come in and listen to what I have to say. I am the master in this house and I am sick of long faces. Now, tomorrow we are all going to Londinium. They have just built a new circus there and we will go and watch the chariot racing and some spectacles. You are all to enjoy yourselves. Is that understood?'

'Yes, dear,' sighed Deleria.

'Yes, Father,' sniffed the children.

CHAPTER 5

The Ghostly Gladiator

Marcellus rode his horse all the way to
Londinium, with Deleria and the children
following in the carriage. The track from the
house to the great Watling Way was deeply
rutted and the family were thrown around
even more than usual, which didn't improve
their moods.

But when they got to Londinium and found the new circus, Clottus started to sit up and take notice.

'Just look at that!' he cried. 'I never saw anything so big.'

'Oh, that's nothing,' said Deleria with a far-away look in her eyes. 'You should see the Colosseum at home in Rome. Now that is something.'

'Well this seems very big to me,' said Twitta.

Marcellus trotted up to them. 'You children seem quite excited at last,' he smiled.

'We're not excited,' said the children quickly. 'We're too miserable.'

'You'll cheer up soon enough when all the racing starts,' said Marcellus, quite excited himself. 'They tell me there are to be gladiatorial fights, too.'

'Gladiators?' cried Clottus. 'Who'll try to kill each other?'

'That's right,' nodded his father.

'Cor!' said Clottus.

'We've got the best seats,' Marcellus told them. 'Nothing but the best for my family. We're in the very front row.'

The circus was packed. People were laughing and talking and vendors were selling all kinds of delicious food — stuffed dormice, dates, honey cakes and roast chestnuts. In the best box sat the Roman Governor of Britain, Pompus, surrounded by his guards, bowing and waving to his friends.

When Marcellus came in with his family, the
Governor stood up and acknowledged them.
Marcellus bowed and waved in return. 'Do
you know the Governor, Father?' asked
Clottus.

'Of course I do,' replied Marcellus,
smiling. 'Old Pompus and me, we go back
a long way. We used to campaign together
in Africa.'

'Gosh,' mumbled Twitta and Clottus.

There was a sound of trumpets and two chariots rushed into the arena.

'Clottus, bet you my new hunting dog the black horses win!' cried his father.

'No, Father, the white ones. You're on with that bet.' Clottus and his father leant forward all during the race. 'Come on white team!' yelled Clottus.

'Come on the blacks, look lively there!' Marcellus shouted.

Clottus's team won, and he was delighted.

Then on came the gladiators. One had a pike and a net and the other was weighed down with armour from his head to his knees. Even his face was covered.

The two men fought long and hard. Although he was less well protected, the gladiator with the net and pike was very skilful. Soon both of them were tired and bleeding, but they seemed to be equally matched. Then the armoured gladiator tripped on the other one's net and fell flat on his back.

The winner quickly put his foot on the armoured gladiator's chest and drew his sword. He turned to the spectators.

'Kill him, kill him!' chanted the crowd and turned their thumbs down.

'Spare him, spare him!' shouted Clottus and Twitta, who felt sorry for the fallen gladiator.

Everyone looked at the Governor — his decision was the only one that mattered.

Suddenly Clottus noticed that the fallen gladiator had a mark on his leg sticking out below the armour, a familiar mark.

'It's Gorjus's ghost!' he shrieked, leaning over the side with Twitta holding his legs. 'It's the ghost of our poor Gorjus!'

'That's no ghost,' cried Twitta, 'it's really him!'

'Gorjus!' shouted her twin. 'It's me — Clottus! Don't worry, I'm coming! I won't let you die!' Clottus wriggled free and fell head first into the arena, followed by Twitta, who jumped down after him.

'Oh, Gorjus,' they cried, and hugged and kissed him.

Marcellus saw what was happening and hurriedly got to his feet to address the Governor.

'Governor,' he called. 'This man Gorjus is known to us! He has lived in our household. Please, for my sake and for the children's, spare his life!'

The Governor recognised Marcellus and immediately gave the thumbs-up sign which told Gorjus's opponent not to kill him.

'Let him live,' said the Governor. 'And Marcellus, I congratulate you on your brave and loyal children. Bring them here, I want to meet them.'

So Clottus and Twitta dusted themselves down and the whole family and Gorjus went to meet the Governor as the crowd cheered and clapped.

'I hope this man Gorjus is not a run-away slave,' said the Governor severely.

'Certainly not,' said Marcellus. 'Here is the document giving him his freedom. I had it drawn up only a few days ago.'

Gorjus gazed at the document in delight.

'Oh master, I am so grateful,' he said. 'I hated being a gladiator.'

'I don't blame you,' said Marcellus. 'But Gorjus, I want you to live with us as a freeman and raise horses for the army. We'll do that instead of keeping cattle.'

'Excellent, excellent,' said the Governor. 'We always need more horses.'

'I would be honoured,' beamed Gorjus. 'And who knows, I may even end up teaching young Clottus here to keep his seat on a horse.'